My Best Friend Fear

WRITTEN BY TASH COX, ILLUSTRATED BY NICOLE BOUFFARD

Thank you so much
to our wonderful families, friends, and supporters
who have helped us befriend fear
and have made this journey possible!

jimMY waS SCareD. AND LONELY.

fear was lonely. and sad.

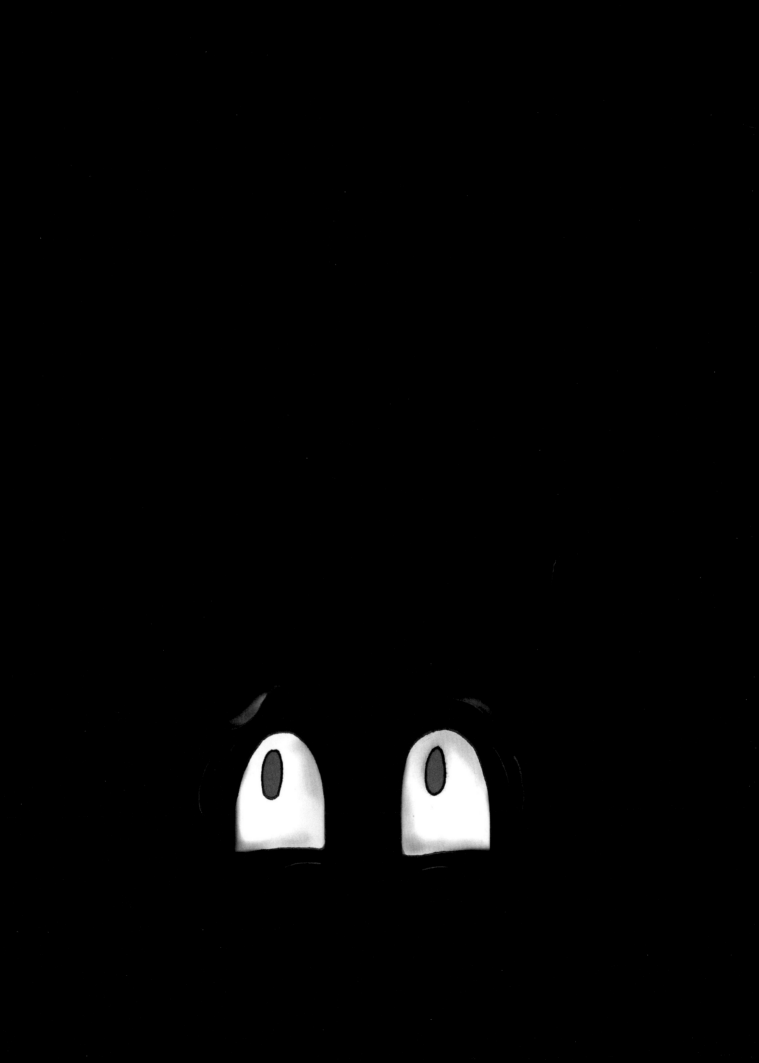

Fear wished he could have friends.
Jimmy did too.

fear WOULD TRY TO TalK TO PEOPLE..
BUT THEY alWaYS RaN aWaY.

jimmy never really knew
what to say.

There were so many things Jimmy wanted to do.
Like slide,

BUT HE FOUND IT EASIER INSTEAD,

TO STAY INSIDE AND PLAY DEAD.

ON SUNSHINEY DAYS, HIS MOM WOULD SAY,

"Jimmy, Dear, why don't you go out and play?"

He would shake his head
and frown at her,

"There are so many things
that could happen out there!"

i COULD get LOST iN THE WOODS
OR DROWNED iN THE Lake!
Eaten BY BearS, FOR goODNESS' Sake!

it's better i stay
by myself
in my room,

'cause no one can
hurt me if
i'm all alone.

- BLE

His mother just smiled
and kissed Jimmy's head,
And Jimmy would
sadly lay
down in his bed.

ONE NIGHT WHEN JIMMY LAY IN HIS BED
HE HEARD A VOICE THAT SOFTLY SAID,

"JIMMY! COME PLAY WITH ME!"

And Jimmy jumped up on his feet.
"Who is here? Who's voice is that?"

"It's me."

Fear said as Jimmy fell flat.

Fear's shadow came into the room
Huge and dark, with horns of doom

"Go away!" Jimmy said,
"Please leave me alone!"

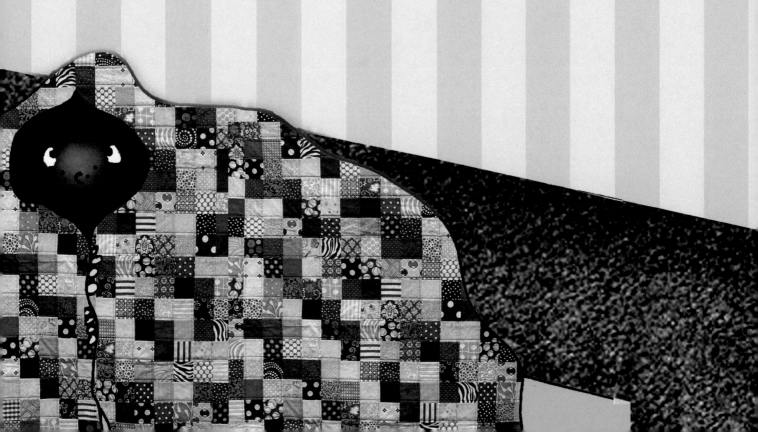

He threw his baseball,
and fear fell with a groan.

"MY HEAD! MY HEAD!"   LITTLE FEAR CRIED OUT.

HE SNIFFLED
AND SNUFFLED
AND RUBBED HIS POOR SNOUT.

"I'M SORRY," SAID JIMMY,
"DOES IT HURT REALLY BADLY?"

"YES, it DOES,"
said fear quite sadly.
"EVERYONE SEES my shadow,
and away they flee."

"AND MY
BROTHERS,
THEY always
make fun
of me."

"...THE KiDS
at School
make fun
of me
TOO."

"SOMETIMES i THINK i BELONG IN a ZOO."

"WHY DO THEY LAUGH? YOU SEEM VERY NICE."

"'Cause I'm scared of sliding

and swinging

and skating on ice.

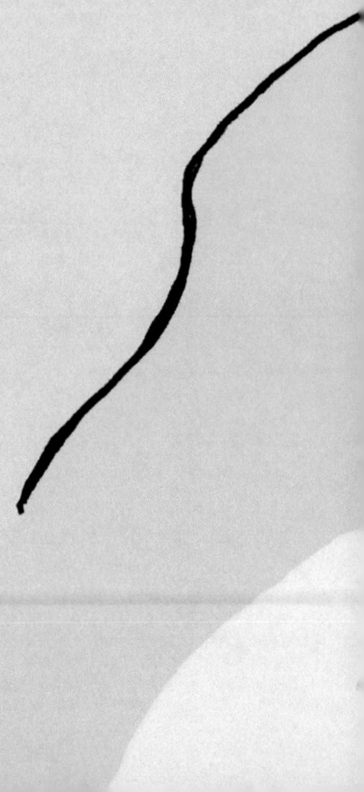

i DON'T LIKE SKIPPING OR RUNNING OR HIDE AND SEEK.

THE KiDS all say
i'M a SCAREDY-cat
freak.

So i'm sad, and i'm lonely,
but that is okay,
'cause i'll live to see another new day."

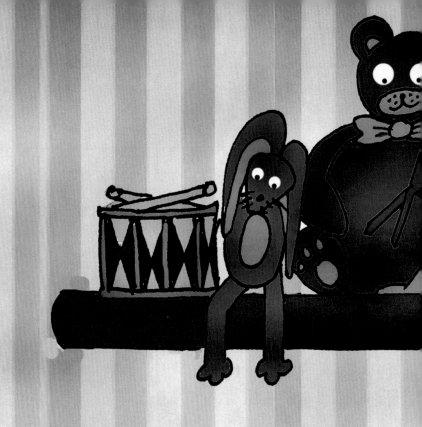

"That's funny you say
you've been by yourself.

i was there when you hid
underneath the toy shelf.

i TRiED TO TaLK TO YOU, TOO,
WHEN YOU'D EAT LUNCH iNSIDE

WHEN YOU'D WATCH THE KIDS SKIP,
RUN, SWING aND SLIDE.

i've been there when you lay
up top in your bed,
i've been in the shadows
when you tried to play dead!"

"You know, now that you say it,
it does seem peculiar.
Your voice and your shadow,
they seem quite familiar.
You say that you've been here
every time i've been scared?"

"YES, i have.
ALL THE SCARY STUFF iS
MEMORiES WE'VE SHARED.

i'VE aLWaYS WaNTED YOU TO
CaLL ME YOUR
BEST, BEST FRiEND,

So we could run
and hide and play and pretend,
But, you'd always ignore me
or just run away."

"i'm sorry that i didn't just ask
you to play.
Come to think of it now,

you're really not scary.
i thought you'd be huge.
And fangy.
And Hairy."

"THOSE are MY BROTHERS, YOU SEE, LiKE ANGER AND WORRY.
THEY'RE THE ONES WHO ARE MEAN AND TOOTHY AND FURRY."

"AS FOR ME, i KNOW i COULD BE a great friend,

it's just my shadow that keeps me from that in the end."

"You know, i'd love to be friends with you...
But, i've never had one,
so i wouldn't know what to do."

"That's easy!" fear said
as he danced, jumped and spun.

"Whatever you want to, whatever sounds fun!"

As fear spoke those words,
Jimmy said with surprise,

"I don't feel scared anymore!
I feel larger than life!"

"You're not scared anymore!
Hoorah! Hooray!
Let's go outside, Jimmy!
Let's go now and play!"

So that is how jimmy
made friends with fear.

THERE WERE MANY ADVENTURES
THEY WENT ON TO SHARE.

They would run in the forest
and play hide and seek.
They would play the kazoo
and skip rocks by the creek.
Sliding and swimming
now all seemed so fun,
But best of all
was when playing was done.

At the end of the day
when it was time for bed,

fear snuggled up
and kissed Jimmy's head.

Jimmy's mom would turn out the lights.
"Sweet dreams, dear Jimmy!
i love you, sleep tight!"

"i love you, Jimmy!"

"i love you, too!"

And Jimmy would sleep soundly
and safely all the night through.

ABOUT THE CREATURES...OOPS, CREATORS!

Tash normally has a fear of bios and speaking of herself in third person. However, learning from Jimmy in befriending Fear, she is a bit more willing to share some tidbits. Hailing from West Texas, the land of sunsets, starry nights, and open expanses of land, she grew up a daydreamer and fully believes to this day that cloud people really do make for the best stories when on road trips or hanging upside down on monkey bars. Her creative life has been expressed in her songwriting and performing arts as a singer in Mankind Is Obsolete, AL1CE, and Alice Underground. She loves all kinds of music and looks at it as a universal way of sharing the beauty of life.

Sometimes she dips her foot in classical singing and met her friend, Nicole, during a Magic Flute production. They are both looking forward to sharing this children's book as a part of their imaginations that has brought them a great deal of joy, helped them overcome fears, and has been a way to connect their friendship through the medium of an illustrated story.

Like Tash, Nicole has had many adventures with our friend, Fear, which has ultimately led to her prestigious position as a soprano of the U.S. Army band. A native of Los Gatos, California, Nicole first learned how to create pictures from her imagination when she learned how to draw and paint from her mom. Her talents expanded beyond just the visual realm and called her to the music medium. Both singer and songwriter, she followed an academic path for her voice, acquiring her master's degree in Opera performance. Nicole loves to create with other artists and ran her own opera company, Orphée Arts, to be able to collaborate with other like-minded artists and performers. Nicole has sung numerous opera roles internationally, domestically, and even exercises her creativity and talent in the realm of bands. Also...she is passionate about parrots and has an adorable parrot named Spanky.

Both ladies have found courage within their friend, Fear, and hope that they can inspire others to also find their courage as well.

55301976R00046

Made in the USA
Columbia, SC
13 April 2019